ADDRESSES

ADDRESSES

BULENT RAUF

BESHARA PUBLICATIONS

ISBN 0 904975 12 6

Published by
Beshara Publications

Printed in Great Britain by
the Beshara Press

Foreword

The point of view from which these addresses are written and to which the reader is inexorably drawn is that of One and Only One Unique Existence. It is this same Reality which the religious intend by the name "God", which is sought by all those who seek knowledge under the aspect of "Truth", and which is the ultimate subject and object of love, called by lovers "the Beloved" though It is Itself the Being of Love. All the numberless interior and exterior worlds are the self-expressions of Sheer Unique Existence, one stage of which is the Godhead, another of which is this most exterior Universe in which we, man, appear.

In potential man is the complete and perfect image of the Unique Existence, but is ignorant of the true state of affairs because of notions of separateness and self-interest. He believes that he exists as a separate entity; even after an intellectual appreciation of his dependence on Existence for his existence, he remains far from realising this in the depths of his being.

These addresses are for those who want to come to understand their relationship to Reality, what their purpose is and how consequently they should proceed. For in wanting to know these matters they have already begun to correspond to their *raison d'être*; as God is reported to have said, "I was like a hidden treasure; I loved to be known and I created the Universes''.

Our wanting to know the Truth is in reality the Truth loving to be known in us, not by something other than Itself, but by that which is Itself at Its own level of Perfect Self Expression, for this is the reality of Man, and our possibility.

That this is not only possible for Man but is indeed his only reason for existence is the distillation of religious teachings and esoteric traditions worldwide. How this spiritual evolution in man is to take place necessarily follows from the unconditioned precondition of the Unique Reality, and is the subject of these addresses.

It would be to misunderstand the situation to ask from which religious, philosophical or mystical tradition the knowledge illuminated in these pages derives. It is rather that this same knowledge has itself given rise to all these diverse traditions, wherever they are found. It is, as Jelaluddin Rumi puts it, ''the same wine in different bottles''.

Bulent Rauf has since its inception been consultant at the Beshara School of Intensive Esoteric Education, formerly at Sherborne House in Gloucestershire and now at Chisholme House, near Hawick in the Scottish Borders. The addresses in this book were, with a few exceptions, originally written for the School's six month courses. The address ''Union'' was delivered to the first annual Symposium of the Muhyiddin Ibn 'Arabi Society held at the University of Durham in 1984.

The students at the School, many hundreds now since the first course in 1975, have derived inestimable benefit from Mr. Rauf's addresses, which were given often in response to a particular stage or difficulty in the course, but always with a clarity and direction which is pertinent to everyone everywhere. As he says himself in one of the addresses, ''The green wood burns with the dry''. Thus we hope that with the publication of this book many more people will derive benefit from it than can take part in a course at Chisholme House. It is the publication for the first time of what is already for the many who know the addresses, a classic of esoteric literature, which should be read, re-read and read again.

Peter Young

Director of Studies, Chisholme House

6th May 1985

Roberton, Hawick, Roxburghshire,
Scotland. TD9 7PH
01450 880215
sender@beshara.org / www.beshara.org

BULENT Rauf was the Honorary Life President of the Muhyiddin Ibn 'Arabi Society until his death in September, 1987. He is the translator into English from the original Turkish of Ismail Hakki Bursevi's commentary and translation of Muhyiddin Ibn 'Arabi's *Fuṣûṣ al-Ḥikam*. A short list of his published works appears at the end of this book.

Contents

1
Sentiment

THIS is a reminder to point out that all that glisters is not gold.

We have all heard that beauty is in the eye of the beholder. Why? – and even – how? Is there a fixed norm or form of beauty to which the eye relates the object seen? But beauty takes so many different forms where one form is often incompatible with another. It must therefore be that the 'form' is a subjective, non-formalised impression of beauty to which the 'eye' relates what it 'sees', and not a shape. This relation then is nothing other than a feeling aroused by the 'vision' the 'eye' experiences with relation to what is felt. (Here note that the 'eye' is obviously not the 'physical instrument' of vision.) A beautiful concerto heard has nothing to do with the eyeball or the iris. In that case, in 'sight' of something which relates favourably to a 'conditioned' feeling pre-existing in the person, the senses register a recognisable, agreeable feeling; agreeable that is, in the sense that what is felt is 'agreeably relatable' to what is already existing as a 'foreknowledge' of what is acceptable as the sentiment of, or relatable to, 'the beautiful'. Thus this feeling is a relationship; and this relationship is a sentiment relatable to beauty. When the sentiment is positive it is satisfactory. If the sentiment is negative in its relationship – i.e. if it is distant from what is acceptable or known as beauty, it engenders either horror, fear, aggression, disgust, spurn or just displeasure. Yet one must remember it is always in relationship, positively or negatively, to beauty.

Keeping this in mind, let us turn to sentiment as such. Each action causes a reaction, but the word 'causes' must be taken warily because we very often find that a cause is merely an effect and that the effect is the cause of the cause. This reaction may or may not be immediately physical; however, any action in any plane has reverberations in all other planes; and non-physical actions equally may have physical effects. This means that these effects must have physical causes, though in turn, these physical causes may be the results of non-physical causes etc. Anger is non-physical, but its effect is physical by creating an overflow of adrenalin, which is its physical effect, and this effect is the cause of the expression of anger in physical terms, such as an outburst, or a fight etc. And the resultant disregard for bodily danger, known as bravery, is again a non-physical effect. Sentiment then, though non-physical, has physical effects, hence each sentiment somehow translates into physical expression. It seems then that non-physical actions, one way or another, give rise to physical expressions. However, this is not always an unavoidable result. Instead of the action resulting from a sentiment giving rise to a physical action, it can so happen that the resultant action is again transposed to a non-physical effect. A sublime example of this is Christ's prayer: "Forgive them, for they know not what they do." The plight of Christ in the hands of his enemies did of course render him impotent of a physical retaliatory action, like striking back for instance; but there was nothing to stop him, say, from spitting back at their faces, or at least verbally cursing them, as so many would have done automatically. So now we can deduce that for some people who can see further into actions, and knowing their opponents' weaknesses, that is to say knowing the premises of their actions clearly, completely and intimately well, it is possible for them to reach a result in the same plane as that in which they are situated, and respond in the same plane with proper effect. But this response in the proper plane can, as we see, only be consequent to knowledge of the premises: a knowledge consequent to a vision that encompasses all the intricacies of the tracings, uniting them into what is known as a 'body of knowledge'.

Sentiment then, without knowledge, is no other than a subjective emotion, unqualitative, unclear, murky, muddy, and devoid of reasonable antecedents. If a child cries because you remove from its reach the bright red, bitter, poisonous liquid which it would like to drink, it is not due to a clear sentiment related to love for that liquid, which is both poisonous and bitter; but simply due to an unqualitative, subjective emotion devoid of any correlation of the premises of knowledge and reason, which, otherwise, would make it clear to the child that this liquid, though red, is bitter and poisonous, and that there are other liquids that are both red and sweet and healthy. Had the child known all these premises it would not cry for the noxious red liquid, but require the sweet red liquid instead. Instead of a nebulous emotion, expressed in tears for it, the child would reserve its sentiment for red liquids both salubrious and pleasant.

This brings us to the following factors: correlation transmutes facts into knowledge as this latter transcends emotion into sentiment. Further, that sentiment, whether positive or negative, is always in relationship to beauty, and equally, sentiment can be either an effect or a cause of an action either physical or non-physical, with its cause or effect finding reaction, reverberation, or simply expression, on one or all planes according to the evolution of the man.

Where there is study of esoteric lore, such as Unity of Existence, naturally comprising the transcendent and the immanent worlds and thereby manifestation, and the knowledge that the prime motive of all manifestation is love, and that the final aim of love is beauty, it becomes inescapable that we dabble in sentiment as we progress along the way. More appropriately named, this sentiment we are most inclined to encounter nascent in ourselves along the way, is the sentiment of love. Like any sentiment, this sentiment of love therefore requires the factor of correlation, knowledge, and relationship to beauty etc., as we have also seen above, together with consequent reaction which is again, as we have seen, expression.

In a matter where we take as the prime motive of creation, or existence in manifestation, the sentiment of love, it is again and obviously inescapable, that we should also have to do with its expression: i.e. love. In these studies on this Way, Love and dealing with love is a requisite.

Let us recall here the story of a teacher who received a would-be student. Questioning him, the teacher found that the student-to-be had never fallen in love, and that there was nothing that he loved. He said to the student, "I am sorry, but there is nothing that I can do for you." Head bowed and sad, the student, a picture of dejection, was just about to shut the door behind him when the teacher tried again and called out, "Wait, is there really nothing in the world for which you feel, no matter how small, a spark of love or special attachment?" The man at the door said, "Yes, I have a donkey of which I am extremely fond. I might even say I love him very much." "Come back," said the teacher, "at least there is something to start with."

At the basis of our primitive – this word is to be taken in its most positive sense – existence, lies the sentiment of love, which we may call according to our 'knowledge' qualified by the plane or level we happen to be in, 'self-love' or the 'egocentric love', or again the 'animal love' etc. etc. The expression of this, in this plane or at this level, is no other than sex. At this distance from knowledge, in other words in relatively complete ignorance, this expression could hardly be anything otherwise qualifiable. One can even say with a great deal of certitude that at this level or plane or – 'the lowest of the low' – the *asfal-as-sâfilîn* – there could almost be no other expression of the Prime Motive of creation, except as sex. It is no wonder then, considering that the great majority of the human kind is at this level, that Freudian psychoanalysis bases itself on the various vicissitudes of sex – and it is right. Even in his subconscious the primary human being is engrossed in nothing else but sex.

However, if you delve deep into the subconscious of most of the human kind, even in cases of the most warped and disfigured sex, one cannot escape noticing a glimmer of desire, but all the same a genuine desire to sublimate sex, though even perhaps as yet amorphous, into love.

But is desire love? The answer is both yes and no. As long as desire is not attuned to knowledge and awareness it is only the first rung of the ladder of expression, thus sex is at the same rung of the ladder of expression. The animal desire, the desire of the sex maniac, the desire of the sexual psychopath are all variants of the 'lowest of the low' rungs of expression. As all expression is the expression of love, since love is the prime motive of manifestation, and manifestation in expression emanating from the original: "...I loved to be known," this is also in some measure love. But it is not love in the sense that it is as yet devoid of that which makes love love, in the right sense of the term: awareness or knowledge. Hence it is an insufficient, or warped or unripe relationship; a relationship so far removed from its relation to ultimate beauty, that it is no longer, so to speak, love. If white is so far removed from white and so mixed with its negation, black, that it is now a dark, dull grey, it is no more white.

Now, as we all know, to climb a ladder, one starts at the bottom where the ladder is placed and goes up, rung by rung, to the top. One does not break off and throw out the first rungs traversed, but they remain for what they are, initial means of progress through which one has passed, and reached or evolved to a different level. When one has reached the top, the surface, one is no more concerned with the first rungs of the ladder through which one went up. In fact, if one keeps referring back to the first few rungs, still in the darkness of the well, one is surely not fully enjoying one's new state of being on the surface and in full light. Enjoying means only one thing: appreciating. And, in passing let us add, if one does not appreciate fully what one has, or what one is given, and this appreciation necessarily includes being grateful that one has that thing, one will certainly lose it, or in other words, it will be taken away from one.

Most of us here are in a new state - we have admittedly all changed since we first came here. In the awareness and knowledge of our new state we must, therefore, not refer back to the same expressions we were used to when we were at the first few rungs of the ladder through which we have come into our new state. This reference back is often not only mental. In many cases it is also physical. Sentiment in us is unavoidably aroused, since we deal with sentiment. But now in our new state we must realise that this sentiment in its further metamorphoses is no other than *dhawq* - taste. But the expression we give to this sentiment must never be, from now on, with a reference to the past; it must be in true relationship to what we now are. Therefore it must be in consequence of our newly-gained knowledge, our newly-found possibility of awareness. If, with this sentiment now aroused in us in our new level or plane, we refer it back to sex and desire for the next person of the opposite sex that has some attraction for us and call this our expression of love we are re-translating the new in terms of the old.

The danger here lies in our comportment which has not as yet caught up, coincided, with our new state of evolution. In short, the danger is therefore in expressing the new level of sentiment with the tools that we were used to employing in the past.

Even if we are not fully attuned, temporarily, to our new state, still, there are other rungs of the ladder higher up on the way we have come, closer to the surface where we now are, to which we could relate. In short, it is an inescapable fact that for us now to refer back to the beginnings is lack of a full appreciation of our new state. This is where we have to be wary, and not to dress all our sentiment of love in a primitive cloak.

A little practice of awareness and correlation is here essential. If through awareness we can correlate certain facts and thus transmute them into a 'body of knowledge'; and then, armed with this knowledge, we can be reassured that the sentiment newly aroused in us can be either a cause or an effect, where these two can find expression either on the physical plane or at the same time in any other plane. Hence it is up to us to give it the expression at the level we desire. If we are people of *dhawq* we give it the expression it deserves, in accordance with our newly-reached state. If we are not grateful, we will give it an expression in reference to the rungs we have come up through, and if we give it the expression which relates it to the first rungs of the ladder of our ascent, we are back where we were.

We know that love englobes sex just as we know that sex is not love. In its perfection, Love is the love of the Perfect Man – *insân-i-kâmil.* His love is universal. He englobes all states and levels. His act of love, his physical love, is no more just sex. His sex is His union. This translated into immanence is the night vigil of Bayazid-i-Bastami. It was full moon in Bastam, an exceedingly beautiful night. Everyone was asleep that late hour of the night except Bayazid. When the early risers for the morning prayer met him coming not from his house, but from another direction, they asked him where he had been all night, Bayazid answered, "It was a beautiful moonlit night and there was no one awake to appreciate the beauty, so I had to go out myself so that His beauty does not go unnoticed."

His beauty in immanence must not go unappreciated. What

the unaware may attribute to the physical union of the Perfect Man in bed is of no consequence. Here is union in immanence; what is commonly known as the 'sexual act' is the physical transmutation into effect of a non-physical cause, which in turn is the effect of His Beauty expressed in the sentiments known as Love, the motive power which activates at all levels. Here remember what He says: "When a man and a woman hold hands in real love, all My *Raḥmah* (Compassion and Mercy) pass through those hands."

May He guide us in all our being, sentiments and actions, and may they be expressed in conformity with our aim, His Union. In short, before each step we take, no matter how insignificant or urgent, in fact with each breath we take, we should be saying what is known as Fatima's Prayer: "Lord do not leave me alone with myself." – i.e. *ya Hâdî, ya Ḥakîm.*

2
Humility

No one is completely devoid of pride if pride in learning is not changed into dignity through humility.

The purpose of all your study is to bring you to a realisation of your 'essential' oneness with the One and Only Absolute Existence. Here remember that the word 'essential' mainly means 'in your essence' as well as your origin and your reality.

This realisation of your 'essential oneness' can only be consequent to the complete humility of your ego to accept this knowledge and make it its own belief; because this knowledge is not the mere acceptance of a 'concept' or 'theory' etc. which may be received by an adjustment of the ego to tolerate, or even to consider this theory or concept or what you will, and still continue unaffected in its (the ego's) separate and illusory self existence as something apart from the basic reality of your 'essential oneness'.

As can be seen when you make of this reality your realisation, you implicitly admit the non-existence of a relationship of the ego to the One or through the One or with the One or in the One or together with the One etc., except that this ego itself is no longer the ego you have known up to now, but the extension of the 'ego' of the One in a single determination, which is differentiation, and which is His individuation as you. This is what prompted Rumi to write the *Mathnawî*, and again this is what constitutes the subject of the story told about Rumi's conversation with Yunus

Emre. The story goes like this: one day Rumi and Yunus Emre met. They had an intimate and very pleasant conversation where Rumi told Yunus of all he had done, reciting to both their delight some of his sublime verse. Yunus Emre was very grateful and highly pleased, but a doubt of personal ability to achieve the same came over him in his utter humility. He remarked aloud: "How true, how lovely; but what a lot of words you have used to say such a simple thing. I could never have done it."

Rumi asked him: "How would you have said it?" Yunus Emre, who was what may be called a 'Folk Poet' replied in a couplet:

> "I wrapped myself in flesh and bones
> And appeared as Yunus."
> (*Ete kemige büründüm*
> *yunus deyu göründüm.*)

What is meant then, is that *you* as a separate entity do not realise, understand or know anything, or, to tell the truth, exist as such. Can your ego, your *nafs*, allow you to admit such a premise? Is it humble enough to admit in all humility that it does not exist as a separate entity, or, apart from being an extension of His ego, exist as such? If your ego does admit this, it has died to itself or in fact has come to life in reality. This then is also *fanâ'* and *baqâ'*. Again, this is death in life. However, this realisation should not remain a mere intellectual and reasonable consideration, easily acceptable in consequence to the original premise of the Unity of Existence. If it is only just this, a reasonable deduction and intellectual comprehension of a logical sequence, then a kind of schizoid existence ensues and what is known as 'realisation' is never attained.

In fact one does arrive at the truth through a logical and intellectual premise which makes one 'know' that one's own existence is nothing but a determination in differentiation which is His individuation as oneself; but that which is accepting and admitting this truth is always you in a subjective appreciation of an intellectual argument as the truth. It can go even further if pushed and admit it of itself as a logical consequence. But if the *nafs* or ego is to apply this reasonable argument to itself as an intellectual premise, it will still retain full autonomy of its separate existence as the judge of the validity of this argument. The ego will appreciate the validity of this reality as an object applicable even to itself but will not allow it to become its own reality, maintaining thereby an individuality of its own which at the same time will intellectually admit that it is an individuation of the One. Two so-called 'realities' conflict in the person, one this intellectual acceptance of the truth, and the other the egocentric, emotional individuality of the person denying to itself the natural consequence of its own logical acceptance. And wherever there is an overtone of emotion, there is a cloudy situation, lacking in clarity.

However, when this emotional self-preservation of the ego arrives through the action of humility, to an acceptance of a sentiment, of a feeling that the truth of the matter is inescapable, the ego finds itself obliged to give way before the clarity of the reason which now fully admits the reality of the matter. This feeling of and for the truth of the matter then takes over the position up to now occupied by the emotion and there is no more room for the continuation of the separate individuality.

The 'loss' of individuality is, however, illusory. The realisation of oneself being a differentiation and individuation of the One Absolute Being re-creates in one an individuality which is beyond comparison; unique; since none of His individuations or manifestations are ever alike, nor ever repeated. Therefore the newly-realised 'individuality' is by all means and considerations more than ever distinctive, gratifying and acceptable to the pride of the ego.

In fact nothing has really happened yet. The ego by effacing itself in humility before the clarity of the reality, has now gained - by admitting the inescapable - further satisfaction and further importance; consequently the admitted truth has only intensified the ego.

Yet the admitted truth also includes a premise which relates this newly-acquired 'individuality' which is His individuation, to the One Absolute Being. Consequently the newly-intensified ego now has to see itself, not centrally - i.e. egocentrically - but as an extension or an individuation of the Ego or the *Nafs* of the One and Only Reality.

On the other hand we know that the Ipseity has imposed on Itself the *Nafs-ar-Raḥmân*, sometimes referred to as the 'Compassionate Ipseity', and the consequence of this adjunction and collusion of the Ipseity as the *Nafas-ar-Raḥmân* (the Breath of Compassion). This self-imposition can best be described by the fact that the Ipseity makes of *raḥmah* - the root of compassion and mercy - a qualification of Itself, and assumes for Itself the *nafs*, the essential quality of the breath of *raḥmah*. It is therefore the individuation or the extension of this very same *Nafs-ar-Raḥmân* which, in its ideal state, should be the constitution of the *nafs* or ego of the individuated self. Now the person, itself, of the individual, has not only found itself not annihilated by its humility, but on the contrary, has gained in intensity, satisfaction and importance to such a degree that it thinks of itself as in the realm of the Divine and assumes pride and grandeur qualified as it essentially is, by the qualification of the Ipseity and the Ipseity of Compassion. But "Grandeur belongs only to Him in the heavens and the earth" (*wa lahu-l kibriyâ' fi-s samawâti wa-l arḍ*), we are told. Now the *nafs*, the ego, must adjust to the correlation of this new factor of which we are reminded. The only way that an adjustment can be brought about is by recalling to mind the two factors, each of which without the other is conducive to *shirk*, or polytheism. These two factors, which like inseparable twins, have to be taken into consideration always together, are immanence and transcendence.

In transcendence there is all the satisfaction the individual, in his ego, can possibly desire: here it finds grandeur, compassion and the eternity of the Ipseity out of which the ego has extended into his individuation; so long as it keeps in mind its essential unity; its unity in the essence with the One. And this 'keeping in mind' of the essential unity is the one and only condition, but also equally a condition *sine qua non*, for the self identification of the ego with the *Nafs* of the Ipseity. This 'keeping in mind' then, is no other than our pre-requisite on this esoteric way we are engaged upon – i.e. our 'awareness'. The moment we lose this 'awareness' we can no longer be conscious of our transcendence. In fact that is why one is often reminded of this by the saying: "The degree of evolution of a person is measurable by the constancy of his awareness."

Admittedly, for the human being it is one of the hardest things to be constantly aware and to be constantly in transcendence, while at the same time one is plunged in the multitude of the distractive atmosphere of life in immanence. Consequently, all the time one is in immanence one must resort to the only factor we have found all through the process of arriving at transcendence and the realisation of the essential oneness of the person with the Absolute Unity. This factor we have mentioned above is the quality by and through which the ego or *nafs* arrives at the acceptance of a sentiment, a feeling that the truth of the matter is inescapable and that the ego or *nafs* has to give way, before the clarity of the reason will fully admit to the reality of the matter – i.e. humility. Hence a peculiar situation results. It is humility which results in grandeur and grandeur requires the aid of humility to regain its transcendence. At the same time, without the consequent grandeur which must ensue if full realisation is to take place, humility is of no consequence. Humility then somehow represents the paradox of a complementary antithesis of grandeur, just like the interior and the exterior, (*bâṭin* and *ẓâhir*) etc. etc.

How, then, does this realisation of the essential Oneness finally filter into one's being, and one is made to realise something which the intellect seems to have accepted a long time ago? It is that any knowledge is a realisation which comes much later than when the lesson is learnt; but this process, as we have said, requires constant, or as humanly near constant, awareness to be the factor of this realisation. Humanly near constancy of awareness is naturally open to many weaknesses of falling back, time and time again, into lapses. It is through this process and sequence of several or innumerable number of these lapses and returns to the requisite humility that one finally acquires a constancy. This process or sequence of lapses and returns to reality is what is known as patience. Hence, with patience, the recurrent self-imposition of humility all the while one is in a lapse, i.e. in immanence, one finally arrives at transcendence. The necessity for patience and humility is the condition of human life and life in immanence: but the person who has come to practice both these near constantly as humanly possible, or in short, is as constantly aware as is humanly possible, has arrived at death before dying (*mûtu qabla anta mûtu* - die before you are dead). He has come to *fanâ'*: and every time he has practised *fanâ'* through humility and patience in his immanent life, he has established himself in *baqâ'*, in transcendence.

But how can one practise humility? Humility is in its broadest terms poverty of spirit; not poverty by lack, but by esteem of individuality; it is the acceptance of one's limitations: in other words a realistic estimation of one's self without aggrandisement of one's egocentrically fabricated self-illusions. In short, it is an *honest* appraisal of one's being, which is tantamount to knowing oneself closely. Though in this close scrutiny of oneself is involved the fullest development of one's possibility in potential, which will eventually bring one to one's fullest perfection, there is nevertheless a hideous and frightening list of one's defects and shortcomings.

One's potential can be sublimated into a transcendent perfection, while one's shortcomings can be dealt with in immanence through a determined and resolved effort to eliminate them. But this latter can only be done by first accepting them for what they are: a hindrance to the development of one's potential. These hindrances may take many different forms. It may be the recurrence of old habits like taking a drug or excessive and possessive love of a parent for his or her child or a love affair dependent on an emotional bias which so intensifies itself that it flares up as a passion where compassion is completely blurred, or inordinate drinking till one is drunk, such cases resulting, although thank God only temporarily, in addling the mind, and befuddling the clarity of vision of mind and reason which are essential for the constancy of awareness.

We spoke of lapses above. If one has trust in Him these lapses should be of no consequence and through this same trust surely to be overcome in time. Seeing these lapses as one's shortcomings is Veracity. When an alcoholic sees his drinking as a shortcoming and accepts the help of the Alcoholics Anonymous for instance, he has come to an honest appraisal of that part of his inner composition which constitutes his ego. Thus this honest appraisal and acceptance of part of one's inner composition, and the consequent admission of this hindrance, is what is known as humility. When an ignorant person admits his ignorance and tries to remove it by studying he is accepting the premise of his ignorance and submitting to the necessity of learning. This acceptance is humility. Therefore we may conclude that the saying, "He who knows himself knows his Lord" means he who is humble enough to face his shortcomings and tries to sublimate his potential in transcendence, knows his Lord. Then, it appears, without humility there is no way one can either realise one's essential unity or know the Lord. "Blessed are the poor in spirit" refers to these same, "for theirs is the Kingdom of Heaven," this last being God's own Kingdom, the Divine Domain: and that it may become yours, you must realise an essential oneness with that same Divine Unity.

Humility is practised by an admission of one's dependence on Unity, so much so that at the turn of the century among those on the Way, the reference to the word 'I' to refer to the subject was considered not only immodest but outright bad form. It was neither polite nor intelligent to use the first person singular, as it denoted a crass lack of humility, and thereby a persistence in non-evolving imperfection. This persistence in imperfection and the consequent ignorance naturally meant the attribution of the initiation of one's own acts to oneself, the uneducated and presumptuous *nafs* or ego. Hence the persistence of the ego which does not evolve cannot possibly come to knowledge and thence to the realisation of one's essential Unity. Even the mention of the phrase "I know...." is persistence in ignorance and lack of humility. This is why the esoteric orders all subscribe to what is known as the 'passing away of oneself' i.e. one's 'I'.

Again one must be reminded that 'passing away' does not mean complete obliteration of the 'I', but simply the relegation of it to its true value, its relative existence in immanence, *but also* its transmutation into relegation to the Oneness and Its Ipseity as Its Own *I*, as we see in the phrase, "*I* was a hidden treasure and *I* loved to be known...."

As you have seen in the story concerning Ibnul 'Arabi's wife, five things are precognised by the people of the Way: trust, patience, certainty, resolution and veracity. We have already mentioned above the parts played by patience, the resolved effort; and the reality which is veracity. It is through knowledge which is received by us that we attain to certainty and knowledge, which is His gift in return for our trust in His Uniqueness and Oneness of Existence, of which we are as near constantly as possible aware. One of the major proofs of our awareness should be our rememoration of Him which is His *Zikr*. The certitude is the security of the heart through which we feel the realisation of His essential Unity, and this security, and thereby satisfaction, because one does not go without the other, is what He refers to: "*Ilâ bi dhikr-Allâh tuṭma'inna al-qulûb*", which means, "Through nothing else but His *Zikr* is the heart satisfied."

Again the essential ingredient of *Zikr* is humility. Without the necessary relegation of the 'I' to Him, the *Zikr* can never be His *Zikr* by Him, through His own individuation as you. There *is* no other form of *Zikr*.

If we have spoken of humility it is because of its deep and constant - yes, constant - importance for those who are resolved to make the effort of progressing towards their essential unity. The five qualities of Ibnul 'Arabi's wife and of those on the Way through realisation, all depend and are founded on the practice of humility. *Fanâ'* and *baqâ'* are dependent on humility, and even grandeur. The 'duonomy' of Lord and Servant is based on humility - need one say more? Practice of humility, therefore, is the fulcrum of all possible evolution without which no manner of attainment is to be expected. But there are pitfalls, even here, and the major one and the most insidious one of which is pride - pride in one's humility. This can take many forms, some of them blatant and some stealthy, and some seemingly quite justifiable, though completely detrimental. Such a case is the affliction by inordinate self-imposed constrictive rectitude, which invariably creates an imbalance which in itself is a heinous denial of what is known as the 'Two Hands of God' used in the creation of Man, His Image, His Viceregent, His

Epitome of Manifestation.

There is no scope for pride, not even pride in rectitude, in a love affair; and our way is knowledge and love, which is the inverse realisation of "I loved to be known..." In all humility therefore, we pray that He guides us in our way; He who is the *Hâdî* (Guide) and the *Ḥakîm* (the Wise).

3
The Contraries

It has been noticed that through your studies and through the lectures you hear you come to conclusions which you find contradicted by other readings and lectures. Consequently certain assertions and predictions will seem puzzling and hence confusing - to say the least - if not unsatisfactory.

You know very little yet, therefore - and this is for your own good - do not attempt judgements upon what you hear and what you read, at this point in your studies - and for some time to come. I am afraid you will have to take what is given even if you find yourselves confused, and blame nothing but your ignorance, because eventually, with more knowledge you will begin to see how two aspects - though seemingly opposite - make one.

Now it is known that God created man in His own Image and that He fashioned man with *both* His hands in the best mode. This use of *both* hands is significant. He does not as He usually does, as we are told, just say "Be" and it is done; but He affirms that He fashioned man by the use of His 'two hands'. Why?

Take the story of the creation of man. It is due to the arrival of man on the scene that we find that an archangel becomes the Devil. We conclude, then, that the existence of the Devil is consequentially necessary to the existence of man. Why?

As we know, in this world everything is one relative to the other and that this relativity of one thing to another is, as

Einstein says, "*ad infinitum*". We know that the three basic principles for a relative state would be space, time and distance. We also know that Infinity is neither measurable by time, space nor distance; how is it then that relativity engenders a state which is not possible in relativity?

There are other snippets of knowledge that have come down to us, such as that "there is no such thing which can really be called a creation", which word assumes that something 'was not' and then suddenly 'it was', and made to come about. Ibn 'Arabi is adamant on this point: there can be no creation *ex nihilo*, he affirms. Why then do we refer to creation of man or creation in general or even talk of a creature or creation? Can it be that what we call 'creation' or 'creature' is just another dimension of the 'uncreated'? Can it be that the 'uncreated' looked at from another, a relative point of view, 'appears', only appears, to be 'created' due to relative vision?

What then causes this relativity, in which we find ourselves, and our vision, perspective and our comprehension of what we see to be so different, so veiled from the reality of things?

There are innumerable queries such as those mentioned above. Perhaps we should try to see things from a different standpoint of view. From, not a new standpoint – because there is no such novelty – but from a standpoint of view whence our vision shows us different lines of perspective where reality and values fall differently and perhaps more true to what they should be.

So then let us start first with deciphering, and then correlating, what we have here.

Our two hands are so peculiarly formed that from one point of view they are one the opposite of the other. Yet, from another point of view – opposition – they correspond as an exact mirror image, one to the other; but this only when they are in 'opposition'. That is, only when one hand is placed as the opposite of the other that it becomes the exact mirror image of the other – whereas seen from a distance as two hands, they are simply a right, and a left hand, one contrary, in form, to the other.

Now we can then say that what is one, contrary to the other, is at the same time, the exact mirror-image of the other. A mirror image is an image which is outside oneself, and is no other than an illusion, due to a refracting surface where what is reflected is in reality not the thing itself, but its image. With some people this idea is so Essential, so constant in their mind that, as in the case of Ibnul 'Arabi, that person will use only and only his right hand for all functions of everyday life, like eating, drinking, writing, touching, holding, taking, giving, etc. In the case of left-handed people, they replace their right hand with their left hand, and their left hand becomes what we call their 'right hand.'

To come back to our subject, we must therefore say that if God insists that He fashioned man with both His hands, He means that man, who is His exact mirror-image, has in him the reality of the right hand which is He, and the illusory mirror-imageness of the left hand which is the refraction of the true hand, as an image. Hence God then, is the reality of man, as well as man being His image in manifestation.

But we have seen that He, God, is Eternal, Indefinite, Infinite, Absolute and the Reality. Then man is all this, due to the right hand; but due to the left hand, he, man, is no other than an image in relativity to all that we have enumerated as God. Hence instead of Absolute, Man is *also* temporal, definite, finite, relative and an illusion. So if we are looking through the right end of the telescope, we get a complete and very plausible picture of Einstein's '*ad infinitum*' arising through relativity. Only, in fact what we see is that the relativity arises from that very '*ad infinitum*'.

This is where the creation of the Devil becomes, to quote what was said above, "consequentially necessary to the existence of man."

The Devil, Satan, represents all the effects of relativity. For instance darkness, as such, has no existence except as lack of light. The further removed one is from light, or if one is 'veiled' from light by some hindrance, the more one is in darkness. Hence darkness is a term for relative light – a mere relative expression. No wonder that Satan was known as the "Prince of Darkness", a negative existent, a contingent existent, existing only due to the lack of action of the opposite positive existent. If we were to look at things from man's point of view as Einstein does, we would conclude that non-reality, illusion, takes us through relativity to consider the existence of Reality and the Absolute.

The imagery of the two hands of God – and it is nothing other than imagery, for far be it from God, having hands as we have – tells us then, just as the story of the creation of Adam and Satan does, of the relativity of the Universes and the 'exterior' of the Perfect Man, whose interior is the same as the Ipseity. The word exterior, *ẓâhir*, which literally means 'visible', 'observable', 'blatant', 'manifested', is the relative, illusory image of that which is unmanifest, Real and Absolute.

Now we know that the Ipseity "extends without extension into the heart (centre, inside) of the Perfect Man" and this is the *bâṭin* (interior, non-visible, hidden) of the Perfect Man; and that his exterior which is the *ẓâhir* (visible, manifested, etc.) *is* the Universes, the whole of the manifestation. So it naturally follows that the Perfect Man is 'the Keeper' so to speak, 'the Overseer', 'the Observer', and 'the Controller' of the Universe which, naturally as we have seen, is his exterior, which he, the Perfect Man, encompasses in himself.

Equally, on the other hand, there are the five Presences – the *ḥaḍarât-i-khamsa* – the *Ghayb*, the *Jabarût*, the *Malakût*, and the *Shuhûd* in order of descent, descent in the sense of distance from the *Ghayb* which is the unknowable Ipseity. The fifth is the Presence of the Perfect Man in this order of '*descent*', who holds in himself all of the five Presences.

Now note that the Perfect Man who englobes all, is at the end stage of this '*descent*' - that is in perfect opposition to the Ipseity of *Ḥaqq*, the Reality, exactly as a perfect image is fully opposite to the object reflected in the mirror. But at the same time we have to admit that this exactly opposite image in the mirror is certainly the furthest away in the 'descent' - through the five Presences - from the *Ghayb*, or the Ipseity.

We have to remember here, again, the creation of Man, where God says "I fashioned man in the best of modes, in My own image, and then I brought him down to the *asfal-as-sâfilîn* (the lowest of the low)." There is surely nothing lower than the lowest of the low and that is where man is, though he is all the same fashioned in the best mode and in His own image, at the other, the furthest end of all the Presences.

Man stays there at the extreme limit of manifestation with *all the potential of being the perfect reflection*, outwardly (*ẓâhir*), of all of what the *Ghayb* and what the Ipseity is and means (*bâṭin*). He is fixed there inexorably and as Giordano Bruno says: "At the crossroads of the infinite (horizon) stands in all his height, the man." Polarized at the end line of the descent through the *ḥaḍarât* (Presences) — in opposition to the Ipseity and with all the potential in him of being the Perfect Image - and yet at the lowest of the low! Animals, plants, even stones and minerals are in degree above him because they are, in their individuation, complete, their potentials realized fully by the sheer fact of their existence - whereas man is not. Man has to choose to realize his potential and then resolve that he realizes himself through an ascent inexorably made difficult for him by the sheer fact of his relativity and through the fact that man has given life and reality to all that host of 'contingent existents to Reality' through recognising their existence as such, by his association with them, and his indulging in them.

All and everyone starts at this point of *asfal-as-sâfilîn* (the lowest of the low) - lower than which there is not. And to quote Milton in his *Paradise Lost*: "there to dwell in adamantine chains and penal fire"! Unless your resolve is unshakeable by secondary vanities of pride and position, occupation and interest with and in things not immediately concerned with your development in knowledge of Reality, which alone can break the ice of this polarization in the lowest of the low and free you to become the Pole instead of the polarized potential, become the active user of all that potential already in you to reflect Him most perfectly and choose to take, without faltering, heeding no complaints or frustrations on your way, to attempt, with perfect resolve, the re-ascension and return to your source, you will never succeed and know what He means by "*inna lillâh wa inna ilayhi râji'ûn*" (they are from Him and to Him they return!).

The above quotation is often spoken for the dead. You are still in this life, therefore you think you are alive. The reality is that you are not. You are dead, you are asleep. Until you wake up, unless you come to life before the physical death, you will remain in varying degrees or at the lowest of the low, lower than which there is not!

How to do this? Through Trust, Certainty, Patience, Resolution and Veracity.

How to acquire these? Again, through Service, Knowledge, Meditation and *Zikr*. But all this has already been said and has been heard - if you have ears to hear with, and discernment. God the *Hâdî* is the only Guide. God the *Ḥakîm* is the most Wise. "Lord!" said the Prophet Mohammed (*S.A.*), "increase me knowledgewise!" as his constant prayer: "*Rabb zadni 'ilman!*" One can do no better if one chooses to try. The choice is yours alone - either to have the most unshakeable resolution or not - and may God help us all.

4
Prayer and Meditation

It is not of prayer in the sense that it is a request, a plea, like that of the faithful housewife who rushes into the church half-dripping with laundry water down her arms quickly dried on her apron, that I am talking, though it has great merit. Nor am I talking of the ritual prayer, executed according to set precepts, half-understood but duly followed through faith mixed with fear, so that what is prescribed to God be given to God, and have done, exactly as rendering to Caesar that which is Caesar's, though there is faith and fortitude involved in it.

What I would like to speak of is prayer offered to God for His grace and for gratification, both of the one who prays and the one who is prayed to, since all gratitude belongs finally to Him.

At first sight this sort of prayer may seem like a convention, a situation pre-conditioned, a polite conversation, a dialogue of two where the one who prays proffers the formalized requisite of conversation in the forms of formulae knowing they will be received and accepted by that same office as dictated its forms. In this category all printed paper burnt up as offering, all the little scented wreaths of flowers that the devotees carry into the temples, all the songs of praise and hymns chanted in, very often, cacophonous unison, etc., are included. But this is only the seemingly conventional and 'at first glimpse' appreciation of prayer at the first rung of the part-human ladder of expression or dialogue.

This kind of formula prayer has its obvious uses and benefits especially in areas where masses of devotees, if left to their own guise to compose their own formulae, would undoubtedly go, some into excess and thereby error and some into complete mediocrity, not un-akin to a basically tepid devotionalism motivating the luke-warm devotee. Or again, it may fall completely short of expression and finally end in a quasi-evolved idolatry.

These again are not the kinds of prayers I want to talk about. At a closer vision, however, these may be quite the opposite. Because whether it be by turning a prayer drum, sending up in flames a written sheet of paper, or offering flowers or songs, these may be on the part of the man praying a sincere devotional correspondence with his Lord which makes of his seemingly mechanical act a personal act of praise or of grace. This, then, no matter what his act seems like, makes of his prayer a sincere devotional practice, a communication between man and God.

Yet there is another prayer which, in the ultimate man-before-God confrontation, makes of the event a communion. By this prayer I understand standing in the presence of that God which is One and Only and Unique. This supra-monotheistic concept is at the basis of all existing religions very often hidden deep down in the recesses of its esoteric foundation, sometimes clearly hermetic, sometimes forbidden, sometimes veiled and sometimes so thinly veiled that it is blatant.

This concept, however, must be clearly and definitely understood. The monotheistic God may be sometimes conceived as ruling over a polytheistic pantheon. It may sometimes be taken to mean a power beyond and above a manifest duality of transcendence and immanence, or of positive and negative qualities where each, since it is the negation of its opposite, then is in constant strife and war. Or it may be a monotheism of plurality and oneness, a triune singularity which represents both the plurality of the number three and the uniqueness of its own existence. Be these as they may, or any other view of monotheism, yet at the principal basis of all esoteric theology it will be found that there is always a condition attached to the theistic concept. This is the condition of an absolute and unique existent.

By its definition the absolute must be all-inclusive since anything outside of it would necessitate its being a relative concept, not absolute, but nevertheless in relativity to what it does not hold in itself. Hence, it is understood that for the absolute to be, so to speak, absolutely absolute, it must contain its own relativity. This then makes of the relative state a state 'no other' than the Absolute. Strange to think that infinity, which is not of the state of relativity, and relativity, which obeys conditions which do not exist in the Absolute, should be formulated in one equation through the finding of a mathematician, a genius, a scientist. Since Einstein, we know that in relativity every thing is one related to the other '*ad infinitum*'.

With this condition of Unicity attached, *sine qua non*, to the Monistic Ipseity, the concept of prayer takes on a different perspective, a different dimension in relationship. This relationship presumes the existence of a dialogue between the Ipseity and its manifestation as creation. This creation then is nothing other in its reality than the Theophany and the prayer ensuing is no other than the Theophanic Prayer which is the Divine Service, since the Unity of Being is the condition of prayer. It means that the prayer is the expression of a mode of the Being, a means of existing and of causing to exist.

One must understand 'causing to exist' as the sequel to the man standing before God in prayer, in the state of Theophany with and before God, who is present and revealing Himself by and to the form of the one who prays. Henri Corbin says: "this view of prayer takes the ground from under the feet of those utterly ignorant of the nature of the Theophanic Imagination as creation..."

Thus viewed in its reality, prayer becomes the highest and the purest form, the ultimate act, of the Divine Service or the Theophanic Vision.

Yet this is not the ritual prayer of the temple, mosque, church or synagogue, in short it is not the prescribed ritualistic prayer of religions, although the *raison d'être* of these religious practices including the ritualistic prayer are designed as man's media to arrive at, or rather, to provide means of arriving at, this Divine Service. But to do this, it is necessary for the ritual of the prayer of religions to pass beyond its ritualistic, not conformity, but emphasis. We see this happen sometimes, actualized during a ritual. Most prayer, ritualistic and religious as it may be, does allow scope to pass beyond its ritualistic emphasis. It is this emphasis of form in the ritual that binds and bounds the spirit of prayer to the performance of the ritual, not allowing it to soar as a mirror-thought to the Theophanic Imagination but remain within the limits set for it in its form.

There is a situation which all religions prescribe, though set aside for the select and not for the masses. This is Meditation. It is wrong to think like most Westerners that meditation is a regional practice necessitating an extreme Far-Eastern mind, a deeply Oriental attitude to religion incompatible with the Western thought-forms basically emanating from the shores of the Eastern Mediterranean whence some of the major religions of today originate. Even the latest of these, the Mohammedan religion, has it from the mouth of its Prophet Mohammed who himself instituted and made compulsory the ritual of Mohammedan daily quintuple prayer, that a single moment of meditation is preferable to seventy thousand times of ritualistic prayer.

It is easy to see why meditation holds such a primordial position in the dual unicity of the concept of God and man.

Meditation is "concentrated thought, to consider, to reflect", says the dictionary. Where the 'tone' of the prayer is subject to atmosphere, a complete Divine Service seems hopelessly impossible within the realms of relative conditioning which is the atmosphere of our daily normal existence. Concentrated thought, reflection, takes us out beyond the limitations of exoteric relative existence and allows for a moment of intensive thought which can give us the necessary conditions of reaching into, or re-establishing for a while, the Theophanic Prayer, the Divine Service. In this case meditation becomes the necessary atmosphere within which real prayer finds its proper 'tone'.

Many forms of meditation exist and some are not even called meditation and pass unnoticed. There may be as many kinds of meditation as there are people perhaps, since each can and probably does give it a personal twist. It is to avoid such happenings which may sometimes be inappropriate or even dangerous that those who 'lead' meditation prefer, quite rightly, certain rules and regulations which they impose, always allowing some elasticity of course, to be able, in case the need arises, to control the trend, if not the contents, of the meditation under way.

We have mentioned contents. By this we mean the focal thought or thoughts the meditators are given, or give themselves, as the point of concentration of the thought. But the essential point of the meditation remains not so much the thought which may vary, but the concentration, which should be the criterion by which all meditation should be judged successful, or even judged meditation at all. And since this concentration is in the nature of excluding all interruptive thought or action, it can be the main criterion, again, for meditations which do not require the central thought upon which to concentrate, but eliminate all interference from thought where the perfect void is required to reside.

This main condition of all meditation, this concentration,

cannot be overstressed. Without it all kinds of thoughts, noises or even half-caught glimpses of things that interplay into the vision of even tightly shut eyes interfere with the successful progress of meditation. It is with deliberate intent that we use the word 'progress' with respect to meditation. Because, though in time, a more immediate location can be achieved for the poise of this concentration, it is usually through a progression based on intensification of the process of concentration that one achieves the perfect poise. Otherwise, the Zen Buddhist meditation Master would have no need to give the helpful, though painful, whack on the shoulders of the novice.

No matter how the meditation progresses or how adroit the meditator grows with practice towards reaching the necessary concentration, whether the meditation takes a focal thought, is 'led' or is an open meditation, in short whichever kind of meditation it is, or how adept the meditators are, there is one rule which must always be complied with. This is the direction or the dedication of the meditation. The direction taken or given is what in the ultimate will lead to the aim of the meditation.

As I have mentioned above, sometimes the meditator's aim, the direction he will dedicate his meditation to, is the elimination of everything so as to leave him in the presence of that supreme quiet centre, that still-point which is the epicentre of all movement, of action or thought; the perfect void wherein resides the essential relationship of immanence and transcendence. Here is the cup, so to speak, fully open, the perfect flower fully bloomed, ready to receive the All-Creational Impulse, the perfect Theophany, and merge it with the matching creaturial receptivity of the in-flowing Most Holy Effusion. This meditation does not aim at reciprocity but to alignment. It is a conscious, concentrated dialogue of expression of the Essential Existence and, but not with, its image in an active receptivity. At this moment, if it is a moment, there is no time. The meditator is beyond the confines of time which only rules within relativity. He is beyond, is aligned to, in unison with his essence which is His Essence. The only existent there present is the One and Only Unique and Absolute Existent and His individuation as the perfected man. For this extension of the Being into the clear cup of the meditator there can be no extension, since extension presumes space, and space, like time and distance, is a rule and requisite of the relative state and the Being may not, cannot, be conditioned by these.

Nothing really happens. The meditator has not moved or changed; the Essential Being has not reached down or moved or extended Itself anywhere. In that still-point they have 're-met' without ever having separated from each other, they have re-cognised their unity. The 'tone' was prepared by the harmony of the stillness; the intensive concentration without qualification or thought has actively prepared the receptivity of the harmonious place wherein alone can take place the Divine Self Revelation, the Theophanic Prayer, the Divine Service. This is not a re-enactment of an original unity of Being. On the contrary, this is the aim and purpose of the Creative Imagination, which in its reality being out of time, is permanent and *ad infinitum*. Again, this is the sole cause and purpose of there being man at all so that he can fulfill that which is required of him, the establishing of that condition of prayer which is the Unity of Being.

There can be no greater prayer and there can be no superior meditation. This is the apotheosis of all prayer and meditation.

5
Of Tahajjud

DURING this period when so many forms of belief are being exposed to us through lectures and through readings, it is of course natural that the mind, and consequently the heart, strays from the central idea for which we have all come here and variously laboured at, for several months. This 'straying' takes place in the following way: the mind placed before various and varied notions begins to cope with each and all of these notions, assimilating, classifying, learning and realising etc. each notion's significance, and then correlating these with all the rest of the already acquired knowledge one has, and finally arriving at a residual total which is what is known as one's own response - one's own learning and one's own particular knowledge, thought, or if you will, 'wisdom'. In short, at the very best this is no other than what can be called a subjective, that is, personal or personalised knowledge. Therefore beware! This is exactly what we should be wary of, as this is the source of *shirk* (polytheism).

In an atmosphere so saturated with His and Only His Existence, where even the mention of the Name God is used warily, in fact, used only because there is no other word with which we can express the Sole and Unique Being; and where this name God is used by us, well aware of its inadequacy because we know that to name Him is to limit Him, which is the depth of ignorance for us, since we know and are certain of His Limitlessness; and where consequently, for us the use of the word God is only done apologetically; in *this* atmosphere, then, as we said, so saturated with Only His Existence alone, to hold personal or subjective views, to have one's own particular knowledge, learning or response is, to say the least, a foolish, regressive, horrifying re-incursion into ignorance and, what is more, a denial, though tacit, of His, that is *Only* His Existence.

We know this, that none of us here would choose to fall into the heinous state of *shirk*. Hence we must find a way out of this *horrendous* state of affairs.

Our first task then should necessarily be to hold vivid in our minds the best reference we know to the Unity of Existence – i.e. not that Existence is only unified in one-ness, but that essentially there is no other existence or existent than the One and Only, the One and the Unique (*Wâḥid-al-Aḥad*). This double way of understanding the Unity of Existence with special emphasis on the second part of the sentence – i.e. the non-existence of anything but the Existence of Only the One and the Unique – should be indelibly printed before our eyes and stressed in our thoughts at all moments and under all considerations.

Before going further, let us notice that the only practice left out here is meditation. Now, you have been told of the practice of *tahajjud*. This is a practice, as we have said before, which helps us in taking us through the *ḥaḍarât*. It is a practice used in many of the *Tarikas* (Ways) of esoteric development. Hence it is very useful to know what it is for. The *Tarikas* (Ways) as such, take the learner, the *murîd*, step by step from the bottom rung of the ladder upwards in his or her esoteric evolution, just like so many of the forms of esoteric evolution precognised by so many systems we have seen, and shall see through the kind exposition of the lecturers that come all the way to this wilderness of Gloucestershire in the dead of winter, to give us an insight into their own different ways of esoteric progression. We are truly thankful to them, because they help to increase us in knowledge.

Incidentally, notice that we did not say "increase our knowledge" but "increase us in knowledge" because this is the real way of understanding that constant prayer of the Prophet Mohammed: "*Rabb zadni 'ilman*" – "Lord increase me knowledge-wise" or as we say "increase me in knowledge", because in the word '*zad-ni*' the suffix '*ni*' added to the root '*zad*', which means increasing, gives the meaning of 'increasing me', the *-ni* suffix being that of the first person singular. Consequently it, the suffix *-ni*, does not refer to knowledge but applies to the root 'increase'. This plea we should repeat constantly during our week of work and living: "*Rabb zadni 'ilman!*" – all knowledge is His for He is the Only Knower, the '*Alîm*, since again according to that Unity of Existence there is only Him and no other.

But to come back to where we left off – i.e. the practice of *tahajjud*, and meditation in general, there are three sayings of the Prophet Mohammed on meditation:

1. "One moment of meditation is more beneficial than a year of (devotional) prayer."

2. "One moment of meditation is more beneficial than seventy years of (devotional) prayer."

3. "One moment of meditation is more beneficial than a thousand years of (devotional) prayer."

We shall quote here the interpretation that Abdul Qadir Gilani gives to this third version of the prophetic saying:

"He who thinks of the Divine Knowledge, wants to have a complete gnosis towards God; the meditation he takes is equal to a thousand years of (devotional) prayer. The real 'gnostic-knowledge' is this. What I mean by saying gnostic-knowledge is the 'state of Unity'. The gnostic reaches the Person for whom he desires gnosis, his Beloved, through this. The result of this state is, in a spiritual way, to fly up to the Universe of Complete Closeness."

This is then the direction required of meditation. In fact, the direction of meditation should at all times be that of His Unity (*tawḥîd*), His Unified state, that is, from His multifarious individuations to His state of Unity, His Oneness, His *Aḥadiyya*, His state of being the *Wâḥid-al-Aḥad*, His state of being the One and the Unique.

But concerning *tahajjud* meditation, we said that it will help take you through the *ḥaḍarât* – the Presences. This is why, for those who have chosen to go step by step up the rung of evolution, this practice is used to take them up through the *ḥaḍarât*, step by step. For us, here, who are concerned only with Him and His Unity, the *ḥaḍarât* are not stages we have to go through; they are presences of the Name *Ẓâhir*, the Manifest, made to come into being according to the nature (the *meshiye*) of the substantial Universe, as the image of the invariable (or fixed) potential (or *'ayn*) represented by that Name.

Indeed, we are, as His individuations, a part of that expression. But in Reality, the expression is no other than a part of our individuation, since our immutable potential is His extension without extension, of His *Bâṭin*, His Interior, the interior of the Perfect Man, whose exterior is the *Ẓâhir*. With this in mind we are not any more concerned with the Presences of descent culminating in the *Alemi Shuhûd* or the *Alemi Mulk*. We are concerned with our intimacy with Him, not in devolution in stages which come down to the individuation, but in the unification of this individuation with His Unity – and *this* is *tawḥîd*!

It would be appropriate here to mention the *Hadîsi Kutsî*: "My servant, if you desire to enter into My intimacy, do not pay attention to the *Mulk* (in other words, the *Shuhûd ḥaḍra*), the *Melekût*, or the *Jebberût*..." There is a quote on this from Gilani which says: "Whoever is satisfied with any one of these (the *ḥaḍarât*), they are expelled from the Company; at the level of God it is thus. I mean to say they have lost the right of Closeness to the Divine Ipseity. Their degrees (of ascension) are stopped. But they had desired Closeness; they cannot reach that Universe in this state. Because they did not desire the thing that was essential....They had only one wing."

As we see we have to be extremely careful not to hold our presence in, or be satisfied with, our penetration into one or all the *ḥaḍarât*; because from the start our declared aim was Union and that of Closeness, that of the *Muqarrabin*. Consequently, during the meditational practice we must be very careful not to think of visiting the *ḥaḍarât* or reaching them, but going through them to further levels, which is the *Ghayb* and the *Ghayb* only, if in our minds this word *Ghayb* means the Ipseity.

The *tahajjud* is an optional practice. Therefore be careful to make of that practice, that very special and high level meditation, a meditation akin to what the Prophet said about meditation (the third form of what he said, and Gilani explained), the meditation of the one "who thinks of the Divine Knowledge, wants to have a complete gnosis towards Him."

The two prayers, one before and one after the meditation, are the necessary adjuncts of such a situation because this meditation is also the *mi'râj* of the person, 'the time when he or she is admitted into the Divine Presence,' the Presence far beyond the *ḥaḍarât* where even angels may not enter. This is the presence of 'Or Less', or 'Or Nearer' (*aw adnâ*), where only man, made in His image and breathed into of His Spirit, – the Result, the Effect, the Cause, the Subject, the Object, the Prime Motive and the Only Reason, the Reality of Realities, that but for Whom there would have been no universes, the Cause of all Mercy and Compassion upon the universes, that which is in accordance with an Extremely Great Nature! – may enter.

There is no state higher than that which man can reach, and the only way to reach it is to reach out for Him and for Him alone. I do not mean only Him, because we already know there is naught but Him in any case. What I mean is Him alone, the One and Only, the *Wâḥid-al-Aḥad*, the Sole Existent. Then reach for the intimacy of that Uniqueness, the intimacy of the Ipseity. When you do that you will find that no knowledge of yours is your personal subjective knowledge limited to your person, but in truth a knowledge at that moment in expression as an individuation of His Knowledge, the knowledge particular to the Omniscient, the One and Only Knower, the *'Alîm*.

If you follow this, then you will find it follows that if you know yourself, as we have exposed above, you know Him, not only as the source of your knowledge, but with respect to the temporariness (in case of time) of your present existence, which is the expression of His individuation at this present moment; but also as you are no other, outside of this temporary, momentary individuation of Him in expression, that your knowledge is no other than His Knowledge - and His Knowledge, like Himself being Indivisible, Omniscient, All-encompassing, and One and Unique.

God knows best.

6
Doubt

Doubt is obviously caused not directly by a lack of knowledge, but a lack of complete certitude and conviction in the knowledge in question. Nobody is free from doubts and doubting, at certain times, during their evolution, and moreover it is a necessary ingredient in the process of 'fixation' of their spiritual 'becoming'. It cannot be a lack of knowledge essentially, because the object of doubt is that knowledge of which one has already had a glimpse. It is not possible to have doubt without first having this initial knowledge, and this knowledge only becomes fully integrated into one's being after having been sifted by the myriad doubts that surround a person and his conditioning.

This is, so to speak, a positive motivating aspect of doubt. However, in this there is a negative quality and action: the *waswâs* – doubt as temptation – doubt, instilled in one to deviate the path of one's knowledge. And it is often so subtle that it is scarcely noticeable, but its effects become magnified and enormous, and one is thus 'led astray'.

It is a wise precaution to doubt people; it is also a wise precaution to doubt oneself. What one must be able to do is to see and judge the Truth in Truth. One must apply that which one doubts to reason and to the intellect. But this will not usually suffice, and then one must ask for His intercession, that one may be able to detach oneself from the whole situation and see the question in the light of Truth, by His intercession.

So the contrary of doubt is certainty, and certainty of the knowledge, the path, the way, that exists before one. And in this certainty the person no longer judges according to his 'doubting' self, for he sees the Truth in Truth. He no longer sees the Truth according to his point of view, for he knows that he does not exist.

Doubt should not be confused with anxiety and fear and other obvious forms of constriction. It is more subtle and devious, it works cunningly from within.

Having been given a great deal of knowledge over a certain period, which one cannot possibly expect to have digested and absorbed, nevertheless, this knowledge received really begins to be part of one's life and one's 'every breath'. It will take time and experience to realise all that one has been given. So now one has the knowledge at present not yet completely 'fixed' and consequently, now is a good time for the *waswâs*, for doubt, to strike.

So what is the antidote to this lack of certainty, and wavering of conviction when it strikes? It is that one must learn not to judge, oneself, but one must discriminate according to reason and intellect, and then apply oneself to Him for intercession so that one may see the Truth in Truth. And this intercession is given to all those who ask; for having brought you 'close to Him', He does not wish for you to be distanced.

There is no existence other than His existence, and the ways to Him are as many as the grains of sand, but to those who have been 'brought close' (the *Muqarrabin*) what doubt could there really be?

Perhaps 'fear and awe' could cause constriction, but that is not doubt in itself, but in the constriction the *waswâs* can find a place to strike.But if you are aware of this you will be able to discriminate the workings of this negativity and learn to take refuge from it in the manner prescribed. To repeat: apply the situation to reason and to the intellect and ask Him to intercede so that one does not fall into the error of 'judging' from the 'doubting self' and the *nafs-al-lawwâma* (the blaming self).

People will also doubt you and doubt what you say in many ways. They will try and undermine your certainty and when you are not helped by those you have around you here it will not always be easy. But that is a trial that you only need fear if you imagine that anything you have learnt here is your knowledge, achieved by your own effort, and you are afraid that it might be taken away. But it is nothing other than a gift and an intercession by Him.

Self-pride is the reverse face of doubt, humility is the reverse face of certainty. And so in humility one is safe, and humility is the pride in which one treasures a gift freely given. Humility is not soft and 'dream-like', it is hard and resilient and will protect one from these doubts of 'self-hood'.

Remember the five prerequisites of the way: Trust, Certainty, Patience, Resolution and Veracity. If you have trust in Him and ask for His intercession you will necessarily find that He will establish this Certainty in you.

7
The One, The Unique

Of the 99 Beautiful Names there are two which are normally pronounced together. It is the Name or the Names *Wâḥid-al-Aḥad* – the One, the Unique, or the One and Only. Both explanations are valid because it means all those circumstances of One-ness, the One-and-Onlyness and the Uniqueness. The reason why these two names are together is due to their alluding to the same reality in two different modes.

The One and the One and Only apply to the dormant aspect which is in other words the non-expressive aspect, whereas the Unique is already beyond that non-expressive face simply because it means incomparable, thereby alluding to a possibility of comparison which it denies – that which is Unique is beyond the possibilities of comparison by virtue of being the one and only of its kind. By its Onlyness it denies similarity or comparability, by its Oneness it refers to its intrinsic loneliness far removed from and beyond any qualification or possibility of qualification and comparability. The two names define the limits and non-limitations of each other and their Uniqueness and Oneness for all time from all time. They are like Janus the Roman god with two faces on one head, which probably is a degeneration from the very same original knowledge of the esoteric being – one looking into the house, the other to an outer extension of its own interior being.

This One, the *Wâḥid*, is the God to which refers the Name *Allâh* in its transcending meaning. The word *Allâh* also refers, in its more immanential meaning, to God-head from whence emerge all the Names, including this very unnameable One, the One and the Unique.

Together, the One and the Unique form, not so much a polarity of two differences, as the one-ness of the twoness (the *ithnâniyyah*) which as two-ness of the One and the Unique represents as yet no number and consequently no plurality.

The plurality stems from the addition of a third aspect of the two, as a progression from the two by a suggested or hinted possibility which is negated at the outset. Therefore plurality, though apparent, is inexistent in so far as its possibility is negated by the Uniqueness of the One. This illusion of plurality, though negated by the pure affirmation of its being the only one of its kind, Unique, remains as an illusory possibility in the observation of the apparent plurality which the immanence seems to represent. That is why the gnostics say that the immanence (*kawn*) is an illusion (*khayâlun*) and/but (*wa*) it is The Truth in Reality (*huwa al-ḥaqq fi al-ḥaqîqah*).

The *a'yân-i-thâbita*, the established potentialities or the yet non-emerged sources whence potentialities may flow, are in the mentations of the Being of the One, the Unique. They are all concentrated in the *Aḥadiyyatu-l-'Ayn*, the Uniqueness of the potential. When due to the mentation of the One Being they acquire being in themselves, by 'contagion', so to speak, the potentialities, concentrated in the Uniqueness of the Potential, demand expression as possible, individuated, and thereby established beings, as potentialities and their consequent expression.

Now know it that *Jamâl*, Beauty, which is God, *Allâh*, the Transcendent and the Immanent, grants their demand out of Essential intrinsic *Raḥmah*, His Benevolence which is All-Pervading as it is the Nature (*Nafs-ar-Raḥmân*) of Beauty which is naturally so inclined, since Beauty cannot be conceived as such if it were otherwise.

The images of these Established Potentialities are, then, what forms the illusion of plurality, the immanence, which as we have seen is illusory, but True in Truth (*Ḥaqq*, the One). Illusory because they are no other than the 'contents' so to speak of the *Aḥadiyyatu-l-'Ayn*, the Uniqueness of the Potential in individuated, particularised possibilities, each possibility representing its own particular potential.

In consideration of this, to think of Plurality where all the plurality emanates from the One and the Unique infinite potential is to ignore and negate the Source of them all as the *Wâḥid-al-Aḥad*.

Of the *Wâḥid-al-Aḥad* it is the face which is the *Aḥad* from where the plurality begins to fade away like a veil of mist that begins to lift. He says: "*Qul huwa Allâhu-l-Aḥad*" ("Say He, the God, is Unique") and adds "*Allâhu-ṣ-Ṣamad*" (the Self-Subsistent), and it is for those who still see plurality that this is said, so that they know how to approach that which is Unique – by "that which does not belong to Me". Anything that tries to approach Uniqueness, certainly can not through what constitutes Uniqueness. It must be through what negates in one any idea of Uniqueness.

8
Fanâ' and Baqâ'

DEATH is a change of state. Therefore it can only be expected to occur, not as a finality, as most of us have come to imagine it to be, but as a transposition from a former state to a new and immediate one, where the actual transposition occurs, sometimes, unnoticed. This is the more so in cases of death during life. What I mean is that a very slow, fraction of a second to a fraction of a second photography would show the uncurling and eventual flowering of a plant, but this process would be useless in the case where the transposition into a new state is in question, because in death during life, the transposition is completely esoteric, and an exoteric sign of it can only be observable, when and if the subject of the change wishes to show it, on purpose or seemingly inadvertently, in some kind of action, whether this be in speech, or by a decision or in a physical action.

What then has happened is almost exactly the same situation as when a lesson is learnt. A lesson, any new information or knowledge acquired, is a realisation which comes some length of time later than when, actually, the learning occurs. It is as if one suddenly was aware that one knew a certain thing to be so. It does not show, except in subsequent action, speech or decision.

When we begin to know ourselves, we change from one state to another until we come to a point of reality which is unchangeable – this is the point of Truth (*Ḥaqq*) which, being non-relative, does not change. Now understand this well –

imagine that we go through wet ground, boggy ground, marsh, swampy places, then to the shore of the sea and finally we find ourselves in the sea. Once we are there, there is no more change of ground, we are in the sea, the ocean. Now, the Reality, the Truth, *Ḥaqq*, is Itself "every moment in another configuration." However, we must not be misled into thinking that because the ocean is as calm as a mirror today, it is rough and capped with white-horses tomorrow, or its surf pounds heavily on dune and rock another day, or that it is a veritable storm where the sea and sky seem to merge into one vengeful darkness ready to drown, it is something other than the ocean. Its action, its temper, is qualified now with this aspect and now with that, but its ocean-ness, its *mâhiyyah* and *huwiyyah*, are the same.

Truth, the *Ḥaqq*, is like this and if we know ourselves fully we are like this - an unchangeable reality, an immutable Essential *'ayn*. It is only until we get to this point, that we must change, be transposed from one state to another, die to a state to find ourselves in another, and this several times over and over again. Each of these times, it is death before dying, our *fanâ'* (passing away) and there are many of them before we come to the final one which takes us to Reality (*baqâ'*).

Each step of our evolution is a transposition to another state and these steps are described through different media, such as the several kinds of *nafs*, such as spiritual *maqâmât* (stations) or such things as we say we are.

Of these last, the first step, where we are now, is when we say "He is me and I am no other than Him though I am not Him". This corresponds to the *nafs* in education, the *nafs-i-lawwama* which has just evolved from the other basic *nafs*, the *nafs-i-ammâra*. This state also corresponds to the first rung of the ladder of ascension. In the *tarikas* (esoteric ways) the student would have to come to realise himself in his or her *Shaykh* or mentor, before he could advance much further where he would be saying "He is me and I am no other". This self-realisation in one's mentor or teacher is called the *fanâ' fi Shaykh*. After this state the steps are easier. Once the realisation is there, that one thinks and knows that "He is me and I am no other", the progress comes quickly. However, self-delusion or unfounded belief, that is, making oneself believe that this is the case, is neither a step in evolution nor an advance. One must be very careful not to be led into this delusion. But if this stage is reached one can then progress to "He is me". Then, only "He". Then the whole of what has passed comes together in "from Me to me". One never says "I" but one can say "me". But if the student has reached the point of real knowledge, has come into real realisation of Reality, he will not even say "me", because in his gnosis he will know there is no one to say it and there is no one to say it to. This is the state of complete annihilation of the self, annihilation meaning not a loss of the Self, but an absolute dissolution of identity in favour of the identity of Ipseity. This is what is known as Union and this is *baqâ'* which means: "to remain". No more change, though still one will notice transformation, just as the eyes, when they emerge from darkness to light, know that they are no longer in darkness, that they are now in full sunlight, yet take time to adjust themselves to vision in full light.

You will meet with writings which tell you that in *baqâ'* there are such things as *baqâ' fi baqâ'* – "Remaining in Remaining", and these meanings are difficult to understand before one is actually there. It is often not even safe to dwell on explanations of such states because, for one reason, these are states not of change, but tempers in the Absoluteness, and therefore, our relative language can only give an inadequate, a defective or erroneous description of these states, which are really not even states; but 'tastes' – *ezwaq*.

You shall wonder possibly how one proceeds to arrive at these stages. Some *tarikas* give you twenty-one thousand *Ismi Jelâl* as a minimum to start with. Ibnul 'Arabi used to prescribe as much as ninety thousand as a starter. These vary – and they vary according to persons and time. Your work will help bring you to a threshold of understanding, and then you will see which way the land lies.

Whatever the way, the gist of the matter is the love-affair, where yearning must be so supreme that it must be stripped of everything but yearning. The aim of this yearning – but an aim only born of this yearning itself, devoid of everything that could be an aim with, alongside, other than this yearning – is Beauty, the *Jamâl*. What happens there and then is nobody's business at all. This is a station of non-description; even the word 'station' is only used to explain somewhat – only those of *dhawq* understand this. May God make it easy for us all.

9
Matter

MATTER does not exist. All tangible matter is an expression of energy. Energy is indestructible and intangible. Matter is tangible and destructible. The only reality matter has is that it is an illusion. In other words you can also say the reality of matter is the reality of its illusion. Illusion is imagery. The reality of the image is the reality of the thing imaged. The image itself is non-reality which veils its reality. The image itself is non-reality. It is the veil. The image itself is the illusion of its reality. Only totality is real. Any part of it, by itself, is an illusion drawn from that totality.

If energy is indestructible, then it must be intangible. Tangible is temporal; a consequence of time, space, because it can be measured. Non-measurable is intangible, therefore infinite. Matter is finite. Matter is time/space/measurable in the *shuhûd* (witnessing). Its reality is intangible, therefore outside or beyond *shuhûd*. *Shuhûd* is the image of that reality which is outside the *shuhûd*.

If all this is remembered constantly, only then can one be aware of reality. The purpose of *shuhûd* is to bring man to this reality. It has no other function or existence. The illusion indicates reality by which man may direct himself to unity. Unity does not only presume the unification of all that is, but the non-existence of aught but the Unique. The Perfect Man is the exteriorisation of the Uniqueness, thereby limiting the infinity of the Uniqueness. However, the interior of the Perfect Man is the Ipseity which is infinite. The face which it exteriorises is the *shuhûd*-illusion. Its reality is the reality of this illusion. That is why Philo says "Man is *Theos* (God) but not *'o Theos* (the God)".

If Perfect Man is taken only as his exteriorisation, then *shirk* of immanencing the transcendence is committed. If one stops at saying "*inna al-kawn khayâlun*" (manifestation is illusion), one has committed the same *shirk* if one does not add "*wa huwa al-ḥaqq fi al-ḥaqîqah*"[1]. *Ḥaqîqah*, reality, is inclusive of the reality of this illusion. It would be primary to think of the Perfect Man as tangible, indeed equally primary to think of man as tangible without at once immediately cognizing in full certainty that he is an illusion, the reality of which is in its illusion.

There is therefore no time, no dimension, no instance, ever, in which there is, has been or will be a creation *ex nihilo*, an existent other than the Unqualifiable, even with the words unique or uniqueness, which we refer to as the Ipseity.

1. *Inna al-kawn khayâlun wa huwa al-ḥaqq fi al-ḥaqîqah* is a *ḥadîth* meaning: The immanence is illusion and it is the Truth in Truth.

10
The Self-Subsistent (*Ṣamad*)

Ṣamadâniyyah is Self-Subsistence; more, it is being Non-dependent on anything. It is different to being *Ghaniyy* (Rich beyond need), in that it has no concern with, need of, or dependence on anything, Existing and Being through itself Complete, with no connection with other than itself, and with no other thing through or by which it may acquire its complete self-independence. It could be called a description of the *'ama*, the state of not looking outward, which is sometimes called the 'Blindness' or the 'Obscurity'. It does not look outwards because all that is of 'outside' is its inside and there is no outside to look out at other than its own inside. It is the existence of a whole which is its own Oneness, and it depends on nothing in all existence - which in fact is His own existence alone - for its existence, except what it is, what it always will be, and what it always has been from all eternity. The reason why it might be called a description of the *'ama* is simply that *'ama* is a non-qualifiable state which is unknowable, whereas the *ṣamadâniyyah* is a quality which describes a state very akin to the *'ama* except that it is qualified by its own self-subsistence. In fact it is the same One Being which has 'descended' from its unqualifiable unknowableness to the state of God-head where qualification starts, yet where this One is only qualifiable by its own self-existence and self-subsistence, untouched by anything other than the very subsistence of itself from all eternity to all eternity.

He says: "Say, He the God is Unique, the God who is Self-Subsistent...", and because the Unknowable and the Unqualifiable is now the source of manifestation, He describes Himself and asserts His Self-Subsistence by saying that He exists only through His own Self-Subsistence, unbegotten, and because of His manifestability as the Self-Subsistent Being, He confirms that He does not beget. Then returning to His original premise of Uniqueness, that there could be nothing like Him or other than Himself, He adds there is not one similar or equal to Him. This is the *sûra* of *Ikhlâs*, the *sûra* of 'Purity' as it is known, or better, it is the *sûra* of Liberty - for no dependant, no matter how little dependent, is entirely free or can be as free as the *ṣamadâniyyah*, which is completely and utterly independent of all imaginable or beyond-imaginable dependence on any thing other than itself in absolute freedom.

Now all the attributes, the Divine Names, are the tools, colourings, means and instruments of manifestation of the One and Unique Being as its own relativisation. Expression of any thing is its relativisation, first and foremost because the expression of a thing is relative to the thing itself - and from there on everything is one relative to the other '*ad infinitum*' as Einstein is said to have said, where the '*ad infinitum*', because '*infinitum*' is not relative, brings everything back, full circle, to the Absolute. This is the way of the Absolute and this is the way of the *Ṣamad*, the Self-Subsistent, as a Name, as a qualification of the Divine One and Unique.

Now know that this image of the Absolute, the *Ṣamad*, has come to the state of manifestation because He, the One, the Unique, the Unknowable, the Unqualifiable, the Absolute, has fashioned the Man, you, in His own image with both His hands - i.e. with all His own potentials. In other words, with all the qualities and states of His own Absoluteness as His own expression, hence as His own Image, bearing in your self all His potentialities including the *ṣamadâniyyah*. This is so because through your origin and Reality you are His complete and Perfect image – even though you are also His relative image since you are His expression, and as He has fashioned you out of the mud and water of this terrestrial globe, you are of His Immanence in His Universe – and His immanence is His Ipseity of *Raḥmân*. Hence Self-Subsistence has to be liberated from the demands of terrestriality and territoriality and relativity.

Since the Perfect Man potential is in you and according to which you have been fashioned in His Image, you have to arrive at a Perfection of imaging Him to be able to acquire all the ninety-nine qualities and attributes in yourself. Then, when the image is perfected and mirrors that which you represent, you will know what *Ṣamad* means.

Ismail Hakki Bursevi (may God be pleased with him, and whose mysteries God has sanctified), says "only he who is the perfect servant knows the freedom of the *ṣamadâniyyah*".

Perfect Service is perfect and total abnegation of the partial human freedom and independence in favour of service to the One, the Unique. Complete servitude is the only factor which negates a separate existence from the one served, simply because the perfect servant is imbued with the qualities and attributes of the One served, without which the service cannot be perfect – as how can service be perfect if the servant does not feel, know, what is the state, the quality, of the One served? Guesswork is surely not as certain and perfect as complete identity with the One served.

It is said that in answer to the demand of Bayazid-i-Bastami as to how he could approach Him the best, God told him that it was through humility and dependence that this could be achieved. Humility is the subjugation of the self to a state of non-being of the 'I' which separates, encapsulates, falsely magnifies the individual which in reality is only His individuation. Conscious of his origin, with the dignity therein implied, if the individual wishes to restitute to that which is the Lord of his individuation the individuality that truly belongs not to himself, then he must subject himself to that Lord. The only way to achieve this is to identify with the Lord, and the only way to identify with Him is through serving that Lord, and thereby becoming intimate to a degree of identity with Him. This can only be done if there is the brand of Union burning in the heart, the Union with the Source of his individuation, with Him whose individuation he is. Another writing on Ismail Hakki Bursevi's tomb reads: "Only those who have the love of Union branded in their heart bring light to the tomb of Bursevi."

All this brings us from humility, by way of Perfect Servanthood, to dependence. Surely Perfect Servanthood necessitates complete dependence on the Lord, because any independence of the self would interfere and prevent the perfection of service through its differing identity to the identity of the Lord. So we see that the way to the freedom of the Absolute Self-Subsistence and Absolute Non-Dependence is only through non-dependence in any way on one's own self, but complete dependence on the Absolute Non-dependence, in fact the Independence, the Freedom of the Self-Subsistent Himself, through that evolution into the identity and intimacy with the Lord, which is Union.

There have been squabbles among the doctors of religion concerning the possibility of a creature, man, holding in himself all the Beautiful Names, some of which are seen to be relegated entirely to God. *Ṣamad* is one of these, and they maintained that this was beyond the reach of man, as no man as such can pretend to Self-Subsistence, since he is dependent on Him who is the *Ḥaqq*, and that a man may not be named even by this attribute. Ibnul 'Arabi refuted this idea simply due to the fact that if man in Perfection, thereby in Union, could not have all the attributes of Him whose image he is, then he would be another than the original, and that would certainly be *shirk*. Equally, the Union mentioned above could not come about if all the potential and attributes were not there, but some left out. For the Union is the result of shedding the notion of otherness from oneself and subsisting only through the subsistence of the Self-Subsistent. Any other kind of being which exists through a subsistence other than the subsistence of the Self-Subsistent, cannot, can never, be in Union. God the *Raḥmân* make it easily possible for His servant as He is the *Laṭîf bi-l 'ibâdi* – "delicate and abundant giver of gifts to My servants."

11
The Raḥmân

"The quality of mercy is not strained,
It droppeth as the gentle rain from heaven
Upon the place beneath: it is twice blessed;
It blesseth him that gives and him that takes..."

(Shakespeare - *The Merchant of Venice*,
IV, I: Portia's speech.)

"CALL Me God (*Allâh*)[1], call Me the *Raḥmân*. Call Me by any of My Beautiful Names". It is necessary here to note that He does not say "Call Me God and/or Call Me *Raḥmân*." Consequently, He thus equates His Name *Raḥmân* with the Name *Allâh*, which is both transcendent and immanential - consequently all-inclusive, thereby complete, thereby

1. God is *Allâh* in Arabic. However, 'God' when unqualified by any other adjective brings to the public mind only its context as the God-Head. *Allâh* does not. The connotation of this word in the Moslem public understanding is immediately of transcendence and the God-Head at once. The notion of God in the Moslem common understanding is a combination of the absolute transcendent Mosaic God and that of the Christians where He has immanenced Himself in the shape of a man, where for those who believe in Him, He is differentiated from Caesar by the division of Possession of the World of the Heavens as other than the possession of this world.

According to Ibnul 'Arabi, the word *Allâh* which is written with only four letters, contains a fifth, another *Alif*, hidden in writing but present in pronunciation. Sadruddin-i-Konevi goes even further to ascribe to the four-letter word, six letters with the addition of the letter *waw* - including God's isthmusial being between the arcs of necessarily-so-ness and of possibilities thereby giving an aspect of God to the Archetypal Complete and Perfect Man, a place of existence within, but not as another, the existence of God. This, Philo of Alexandria, roughly before and contemporary of Christ, has already affirmed as: "The Perfect Man is God (*Theos*) but not The God (*'o Theos*)".

Absolute – so that when *Allâh* or *Raḥmân* is mentioned they become interchangeable when no differentiation of aspects is intended. However, since we know all His Names contain all His other Names, it becomes necessary to know why it is that in this case the Name *Raḥmân* has been chosen to equate with His Name *Allâh* and why it is that the quote does not simply say "Call Me by any one of My Beautiful Names".

The importance here is specifically in the choice of the Name *Raḥmân*. Elsewhere again He mentions that He likes His Quality of *Raḥmân* the best. Consequently it is due to this predilection for *raḥmah* that He imposes upon Himself the *Nafs-ar-Raḥmân*, the Being, the Self-ness of *Raḥmân*. There is another situation equally important where the *Raḥmân*, this time as the *Nafas-ar-Raḥmân*, the out-going breath, the Expansion, by Its quality of exhalation expands all that is by position in constriction, into Expression.

By 'position' one understands an aspect of a situation wherein the possibilities intrinsic in them are not in expansive expression, like a painting which has not yet been seen by someone which therefore has not yet expressed to the viewer its potential, beauty, meaning, the painter's intention etc. The subject matter of the painting remains the same as the painter's intention in his mind through the first exposition, through its being admired, then bought, then sold, then finally appearing in the galleries and museums. In fact all the vicissitudes of its travel from the mind to the museum has not changed the painting, but all the while the original intention of the painter has gathered different numbers and manners of comprehension, expressions with which it has acquired expanded loci of receptivity of the original intention of the painter. Similarly the exhalation of the *nafas* of the *Raḥmân* becomes tantamount to expression. This is attested to by Himself when He says in the *Ayatu-l Kursî*, "*wasi'a kursiyyuhu-s samawâti wa-l arḍ*". "His *kursî* extended over" is to be understood as if the *Kursî* were englobing the Heavens and the Earth (*samawâti wa-l arḍ*). Here the word *kursî*, which means a chair, a throne, assumes the meaning of that upon which 'rests' the Being, the *Nafs*, in the same way as a potentate imposes a throne by which he expresses his presence as the ruler of the world and is no other than that very *raḥmah* which, imposed by Himself upon Himself, is known as the Ipseity of *Raḥmân* and whenever it expands, it is the Breath of that *Raḥmân*.

Now, the *Raḥmân* must be understood correctly.

Raḥmah has the meaning of Benevolence, Compassion, Mercy, collectively. It is out of Benevolence that stems what is specifically referred to as Compassion (*raḥmâniyyah*), Compassionate-Mercy (*raḥmân-ar-raḥîm*), or Mercy in response to some demand of forgiveness or need of protection etc. (*raḥîmiyyah*). Note that there is no specific notion of pity or pitying or kindliness involved in this. That is yet another of His Names. The *Raḥmân* is rather like a Blessing where the Blesser by nature of Its love of giving out a Blessing (*Nafas-ar-Raḥmân*) on some object, expands that virtue of Blessing which, though it effects the object, yet still engulfs and englobes, in its own Blessing, the Blesser through its expansion, which coming from Him as the Source, pervades all that is called 'other' or named as 'things' to differentiate the object from the Subject which is no-thing.

Now the *Raḥmân*, the Absolute Benevolence, emanates, can emanate only, from the Nature, the Self, of Absolute Beauty. There is no argument possibly valid here, because only Sheer Beauty, Absolute Beauty – and one does not mean here the adjective beauty or beautiful which is used to qualify an Absolute state; what is meant is the Being of Beauty as an Absolute, all-encompassing Pure, Sheer Beauty – can have in its nature and consequently in its expression the intention of Absolute Benevolence. In fact even without any intention Beauty is Mercy, Compassion and Absolute Benevolence. It is in fact the unfailing source of all Benevolence, because it can only have one movement in its superlative form and the *Raḥmân* is a superlative form of *raḥmah*, meaning the 'Person' or 'Self' which is – not becomes – the superlative form of *raḥmah* as a Being. That movement is called Love. As no love can be imagined without complete benevolence towards the object of love, conversely no love can love an object which does not attract all the benevolence of the lover. It is in the Absolute Beauty, then, that the *Raḥmân* finds its origin and source and uses the vehicle of Love for movement – Love which is the movement of Beauty. The *Raḥmân* then is the Ipseity of Beauty through its Essence, Source and Origin. Then again it is the Beauty in expression equally as the Ipseity of Beauty and its expansion as its ever-expanding Breath. The conjoining of the terms God and Beauty is wonderfully expressed in the *ḥadîth*: "Indeed God is extremely Beautiful and loves Beauty." Here occurs the inversion of the movement of Beauty, Love, where indeed the extremely Beautiful loves Beauty. But He who says "Call Me *Raḥmân*" is Beauty, Sheer and Absolute. Then He who says "Call Me *Raḥmân*" loves Beauty, which is Himself. But then it also follows that He who is called upon to call Him Beauty or the *Raḥmân* is that which is 'extremely Beautiful'. There seems to be only a difference of 'position' between that which is and that which loves it. We have also seen that that which is different by 'position' is completely expanded by the Benevolence of Beauty through its *nafas-ar-raḥmân*. The painting has travelled to the museum to the gaze and appreciation of all. The masterpiece, the painting, is then a self-portrait where its nature is the *nafs-ar-raḥmân* and its expanding into the vision, comprehension, the appreciation of all that see it, is through the *nafas-ar-raḥmân*.

Otherwise said, Sheer Beauty through its intrinsic Benevolence of Nature (the *nafs-ar-raḥmân*) has imposed upon Itself to show Itself to the Universes, and the Universes which in a 'position' of Being have been expanded to objective existence to see that which is exposed to them and using the same vehicle by which the Beauty came, return the Love, the *Raḥmah* and the Sheer Beauty back to Him which is the *Jamâl* - Sheer Beauty. So Beauty, out of Benevolence, showed Itself to Itself for Love of Beauty, and returned It to Itself.

There must be a purpose in exhibiting the masterpiece. The painter does not hide his masterpiece in the studio which is his Treasury of art. Thus because of the embodiment of *raḥmah* which is the *Raḥmân*, Beauty chose to breathe out, exhale, express and expose all that is in this Treasury of Beauty which is Himself.

Nature is the *Nafs-ar-Raḥmân* from here to the ends of the Universes. Nature, as we know it and as it is, is the very Being of Benevolence. The Breath, the expansion of this Benevolence, extends, englobes and encompasses in Its expansion all the Heavens and the earths. Its movement, the movement of the Being of Benevolence, the Expansion of the Breath of Benevolence, is necessarily through Love. Love is the movement of Beauty and Beauty is He who exposes that Beauty through the vehicle of Love, a quality intrinsic to Beauty so that Beauty is known, is seen by that which is 'other', which is no other than Him as 'other'. When He says, "I was a hidden treasure and I loved that I be known", the one who will know is 'other' without being 'other' since He Himself is the Knower. Then where is that which is 'other'? He, the 'other', is 'no other' than He who is 'other', which is 'no other'. That is why He has to fashion him, the 'other', in His own image with both His hands. That which is named 'other' and yet is 'no other' is the Perfect Man who is all the same *Theos* even though because of that 'other'ness, although 'without being other', he may not be qualified as the original is, as *'o Theos*. This is as should be and it is good taste and good tact and affords no place for confusion. The 'other' can never be the same. It can be 'no other' and then the same, only and only if it has eradicated from itself the 'other'ness – hence not the admirer, lover, appreciator of Beauty, but the Beauty itself; and that happens as Benevolence wishes; and Benevolence wishes. That is why there are all the exhortations, utterances, cajolings, threats, reminders, callings, recallings, intermediaries, ambassadors, special envoys and so-called prophetic functions – since there is nothing to prophesy except to expose the mystery a little more each time as comprehension and the knowledge of Reality increases so that no one is misled by an all too easy assumption that *Theos* is *'o Theos* and no other. No other though it is, it is all the same not the same. Really to get the *Theos* to read *'o Theos* you would have to cut off the quote and re-write, never before having assumed to have written it at all, as, this time, with the *'o*. Because *Theos* is you, you must eradicate that you, to become either 'He' or 'Me'. God the *Raḥmân* is the Guide, the *Hâdî*.

12
Union

DICTIONARIES give the meaning of a combination, an association, something of a collectivity, to union, like a Union of States, like the Workers' Union etc. and also that it has the meaning of unification of different but similar elements, a unifying principle, in short, which unites into one body that which is several or separate.

None of these meanings apply to what Muhyiddin Ibn 'Arabi understands from Union, nor does it apply to what any of the esoteric ways mean by union. Though the word 'union' may mean 'unification'.

In Ibnul 'Arabi's case, or for that matter in all Sufi esoteric lore, Union is understood to equate in meaning to the word *tawḥîd*. *Tawḥîd* actually does mean 'unification',or 'making into one'. But what *tawḥîd* is meant to mean is *not* 'unification' of several things, *nor* is it meant to mean 'making into one' of many things. However, in the idea of 'making into one' there is a possibility of delving into the 'mystery' of the word *tawḥîd* which means 'unifying' into One. This 'mystery', if it is a mystery, lies in the prerequisite knowledge of *tawḥîd* or 'making into One'. That knowledge is that there is absolutely no other Being in existence than the One and Only,Self-Subsistent Being which is not 'All' that there is, but that what seems to be 'all' is no other than Itself, somewhat like the apparently different facets of the jewel are no other than the jewel itself or like the different colours refracted by the prism are no other than The Light which turns into various colours when passed through the prism.

Tawḥîd then comes to mean the recognition of plurality as no other than the fact that what seemingly appears as many or varied is in reality One and Only in Essence.

The meaning of the word *tawḥîd* or Union as used by many like Ibnul 'Arabi (and many that followed him) does not, however, end with its admitted esoteric vocabulary meaning. For Ibnul 'Arabi and many that think like him, *tawḥîd* or Union is not a matter of knowing what it means but the act of progression towards the fulfilment of that action and knowledge, to feel an irresistible desire to reach, consciously, that state of being where one is in Union or in *tawḥîd* – i.e. in the state of having formed a concept whereby there exists no other than the One and Only, the Unique Existent, Absolute, not like a monarch, but absolute in the sense that since it is all-inclusive it is not comparable or relatable to anything outside itself and therefore Complete and thereby Perfect. Yet the knowledge of all this is not *per se* enough to allow one to be in the State of Union or *tawḥîd*. An example borrowed from Ibnul 'Arabi clarifies what is meant by knowing about it and being it. He says one might know what heroism is but that does not make one into a hero until one actually performs an act of heroism. Then only is one a hero. So *tawḥîd* or Union is a deliberate act of progression to being One. Not only is it an act which is deliberate, like any other deliberate action, but that action deliberately and consciously undertaken must, by its nature, be all-exclusive, irresistible in its attraction, a passion induced by the supreme and all-pervading Love of the State of Union or *tawḥîd*. Ismail Hakki Bursevi, who was one of the great teachers of the Jelveti order, now closed, and who translated and commented upon the *Fuṣûṣ al-Ḥikam* of Ibnul 'Arabi in what may be called the definitive commentary on the *Fuṣûṣ* up to now, has an inscription on his modest tomb in Bursa which proclaims that only he who has the Love of *tawḥîd* branded upon his heart brings light to the tomb of Ismail Hakki Bursevi.

As we can gather, Union or *tawḥîd* is both an act of progression and a State of Being to which the action of progression leads but does not stop in its action when once it is in Being.

That *tawḥîd* is both a State of Being and an act of progression without end is due to at least four aspects of the Being Itself:

First, because the Being is Complete, Non-relative, therefore beyond relativity defined by time, space, distance. It is infinite. As Einstein says, everything is relative one to another *ad infinitum*, looking at it from one end of the telescope, so to speak. Then that which is not defined by the requisite of the relative is infinite; and the Infinite is limitless, without boundaries in time. Consequently the ever progressive Union is ever, non-stop Continuous Being.

The second aspect derives from this very same non-conditional. That Being is, at all instants, in a different configuration, and different 'business' or State of Being (*kulli ânin fi sha'nin* – at every instant in a different state or 'business', or at a 'thing that is its private thing', which are of the *shu'ûn-i-dhâtiya* or 'to do with "things" of its own Ipseity'). Hence the Progression mentioned and the State of the Union is constantly varied at every instant to suit and conform to the State of the Configuration in which the Being happens to reveal Itself.

The third aspect of the non-stop progression and the State of Being is that it is irremediably and exclusively a matter of Love. Now, according to Ibnul 'Arabi, Love is a sentiment with an aim to come into *tawḥîd* or Union with Beauty. Hence it is the vehicle which transports the sentiment for Beauty to Beauty.

When Ibnul 'Arabi speaks of sentiment he makes it very clearly understood that he is not talking of an emotion. Emotions are murky at best and Ibnul 'Arabi's sentiment is crystal-clear and definite, even to the degree of exclusivity. This sentiment is an active feeling which is only translatable with expressive Love which is equally its vehicle. Hence Love is the Love of Beauty to which it transports the Lover. The sentiment and its vehicle coinciding in action, in purpose, in reaching to and in the State of Being that which it reaches out towards, Beauty.

One has to be extremely careful in understanding this Beauty, not as something qualified by Beauty, even though we have no other means of expressing it except by a qualifying adjective. Yet we must come to know that Beauty not as qualified by the adjective of Beauty but as sheer Beauty, as Beauty Itself, far beyond any thing by which it can be qualified - a Total Beauty, therefore a perfection which can never be qualified except by Its own Being such as It is. A qualifying statement comes as a *ḥadîth* in the words of the Prophet Mohammed: *inna Allâhu Jamîlun wa yuḥibbu-l Jamâl* - "In that God is extremely Beautiful and Loves Beauty".

The fourth aspect of the continuous act of progression and the State of Being is that it is Alive, *Ḥayy*. Ibnul 'Arabi makes us definitely understand that Life is movement. Water which is not in the motion of flowing, therefore not in movement, is stagnant. Stagnant water is 'dead' water. Life being the quality of the Being, the State of Its Being is active and in movement. Consequently all action towards Union or *tawḥîd* with that Being and the State of Being of that Being are in constant movement. This consideration takes us back to the third aspect mentioned above. If the Being is in constant movement then Beauty is equally in a state of constant movement. As the movement of Beauty is Love, then the Beauty is in constant Love and it is because of this Sentiment that the Love of Union or *tawḥîd* is a constant progression towards Beauty, as at the same time being in the state of that Being is Beauty.

We have seen the constant movement of Beauty and that the movement of Beauty is Love. Yet Beauty is also in constant expression, as Beauty without expression is inconceivable when there is no one to appreciate that expression or to witness its presence. So the expression of Beauty is Love as well as it being vehicled by Love.

Ibnul ‘Arabi states that even in the other world as well as this, man is constantly in progress whether he is conscious of it or not. What we have seen here is that the progressive movement with Love towards Beauty is constant whether one knows about it or not or whether one is in this world or not. In the case of the two worlds the explanation is easy. Ibnul ‘Arabi sees ‘death’ as such, leave alone as a finality, as not existing. He himself goes and comes to and fro to the other world, converses with the inhabitants of both worlds and advises them, and assumes that such a state is not a unique possibility accessible to him alone. Quite in concordance with the saying of the Prophet ‘Die before you die’, Ibnul ‘Arabi expects all that follow his teachings to acquiesce and to accede as urgently and as possibly soon as each is capable of understanding what it means. He has no patience in this and will brook no reluctance. He says in his *Treatise on Being* (*Risâlat-ul Wujûdiyyah*) that he has no converse with those who see illusion as reality since they are limited in their vision to the objects or ‘things’ seen and are veiled from Reality. They are not, therefore, ardently in Love and are not consequently intent on Union or *tawḥîd*.

As regards man’s progression towards Union or *tawḥîd*, since Beauty is always in expression and Love is Its movement, then the expression which is always in movement cannot but reach man for whom that movement and that expression is meant. Whether man acknowledges this or not, he is subjected to that Love and Beauty. And the effusion of Beauty is such that it covers the wary and the unwary recipient, the former consciously responding to it, the latter denying it through unawareness. But when he is in the other world, released from the veil of his relative identity, he will see the Reality of the situation necessarily and will comply and conform with the unavoidable Truth (*Ḥaqq*) - eventually reaching a state which will be his state of unconscious but definite progress. This progress might be of many varieties and kinds but it is always a progress either through and to Divine Names or even further to the Essential Being and the Perfection of Being. That will depend on many factors to do with his ability to receive the Divine Effusions and his appreciation of the Beauty. When Ibnul 'Arabi says everyone progresses he does not equally say everyone progresses in the same latitude nor in the same manner. This is possible because though the Divine Names are the source of relativity they are all the same absolute in their Essence emanating from the same Ipseity.

It is true that the way one goes, towards Union - *tawḥîd* - or not, and which way, is a matter of Taste (*dhawq*). The Progress through Taste (*dhawq*) does not impair in any way the Expression of Beauty nor the Love.

In his *Fuṣûṣ al-Ḥikam*, Ibnul 'Arabi quotes a converse where David is told: "Oh David, it is I who desire them even more intensely" than they yearn for Him. So as we have seen Divine Love remains constant, only response to it is relative depending on many factors, one of which is ability to receive, then the inclination to respond and to return. Then acceptance or denial of Love depends on the individual's desire to wake up to that Reality of Beauty or not. This is a complicated matter and that is why it is referred to as a mystery.

To 'wake up' or not is, as we have seen, a matter of Taste (*dhawq*). It is related that Bayazid (also referred to as Abu Yazid) of Bastam in Iran, one of the greatest Saints of this line of thought, was met by some people going to the mosque for the pre-dawn prayer. Bayazid of Bastam was coming from a direction other than his house. Upon being questioned as to where he had been so early, Bayazid answered that it had been an especially lovely moonlit night and everyone was asleep, so he had decided, since God had been so bountiful in showing His Beauty, that at least he himself should devote his night to the witnessing of such loveliness, as no other servant of God seemed to wish to do, and had passed the night in wakeful adoration of Beauty, so that His Beauty did not pass unnoticed.

To be conscious or awake to Beauty is a matter of predilection in the servant. The servant of a master or Lord (*Rabb*) is necessarily advanced in the perfection of his function in the ratio of his self-identification with the Lord he serves.

Though service itself does in no way belong to the Lord, service of the Lord entails full identification with the Lord served, so as to serve in the best manner possible. This self-imposed humility to serve the Beloved has its side of dignity, which is the dignity of the knowledge that one is willingly serving the supreme Beauty. Elsewhere we have said (in the film called 'Turning') that Love is a bondage willingly accepted by the free, and it is this willingness, this choice to serve that Beauty in Love, that is what imparts dignity to the office. Again Ibnul 'Arabi says in the Tuesday recital of his *Wird* (a collection of daily recitals he wrote for his pupils) "and dress me in the cloak of Dearness and Receiving... and crown me with the crown of Generosity and Dignity".

So through service with dignity and seeing oneself from the point of view of God, not from the point of view of the self itself until one is Him and not oneself (Saturday recital of the *Wird*) and demanding to be clothed with the Cloak of Beauty and being crowned with the crown of Awe and Majesty (Friday Evening recital), the servant finds identification with the Lord he serves. This is how "*Tawḥīd* is the Mystery of Servanthood' (*Wird*: Sunday recital)."

As Ibnul 'Arabi says in his *Kernel of the Kernel*, when the servant has gathered in himself the five states of awareness, then he becomes a Sufi, a gnostic (*'ârif*). After this state, Ibnul 'Arabi says "five other thing happen, the explanation of which is not suitable here and to reveal this even is forbidden." Elsewhere there is a passage in the *Kernel of the Kernel* where is described what happens to the servant after he has reached *fanâ'* (the state of non-existence as oneself as mentioned in the *Wird* above: "...until there be You and not I") where after a while the servant is "painted with the Divine colour" and "God grants him an existence from His own existence." "Then God gives this man of knowledge a Divine Sight, Ear, Tongue..." A person's "real understanding and knowledge starts after this".

Nothing has happened. Simply, that he who was Essentially Him, came to realise, but not only intellectually, that he was no other than Him.

As we have seen the prerequisite of this unceasing progression towards and finally Being is a predilection of those who have the good-Taste for it. As the French saying goes "*le bon-goût s'apprend*" (good-taste is learnt) and as the Prophet Mohammed said: "give me Taste in vision", the crux of the matter of Union or *tawḥîd* seems to lie in a taste for it. *Dhawq* (taste) has a connotation of 'enjoyment' in it. There is 'joy' in the enjoyment of it because it leads to appreciating fully, and then identifying with, Beauty.

The drunken Sufi poet of Iran wrote:

> Here with a loaf of bread beneath the Bough,
> A flask of Wine, a Book of Verse - and Thou
> Beside me singing in the Wilderness -
> And Wilderness is Paradise enow.

The Bread is the body of Knowledge. The Verse is the Praise of Beauty. The Wine is its intoxication and Thou art Thou. Beneath a bough is in this world, already here, it is

Paradise - if one has the predilection and the necessary intention to progress towards and Be no other than that which is unqualified Sheer Beauty, the *Jamâl*.

The Turkish poet wrote "*Kande baksan ol güzel Allahi gör!*" - "Wherever you look see that Beautiful God!"

No other can see God. But those who have vision to see 'no other' see God in all His effects everywhere. When one's vision has progressed to a vision of 'no other', then one sees Him everywhere. From thence, as Ibnul 'Arabi says in his poem:

> O marvel!.......I follow the religion of Love:
> Whatever way Love's mounts take,
> That is my religion and my faith.

This is seeing Him everywhere; whatever way Love transports, it is necessarily to Beauty and that is his religion and his faith.

A SHORT BIBLIOGRAPHY

Translations

Fuṣûṣ al-Ḥikam — Ismail Hakki Bursevi's Translation of and Commentary on Fuṣûṣ al-Ḥikam by Muhyiddin Ibn 'Arabi, rendered into English by Bulent Rauf with the help of R. Brass and H. Tollemache, Muhyiddin Ibn 'Arabi Society, Oxford and Istanbul, Vol 1 1986, Vol 2 1987.

Kernel of the Kernel — Ismail Hakki Bursevi's Translation of Kernel of the Kernel by Muhyiddin Ibn 'Arabi, translated from Turkish by Bulent Rauf, Beshara Publications, 1981.

Mystical Astrology According to Ibn 'Arabi by Titus Burckhardt, translated from the French by Bulent Rauf, Beshara Publications, 1977.

Own writings

Addresses, Beshara Publications, 1987. *Eleven addresses originally written for students of the Beshara School of Intensive Esoteric Education, together with the paper "Union and Ibn 'Arabi".*

Union and Ibn 'Arabi, *Journal of the Muhyiddin Ibn 'Arabi Society,* Vol III, 1984.

Universality and Ibn 'Arabi, *Journal of the Muhyiddin Ibn 'Arabi Society,* Vol IV, 1985.

Wisdom and Wisdoms, *Journal of the Muhyiddin Ibn 'Arabi Society,* Vol V, 1986.

Concerning the Universality of Ibn 'Arabi, *Journal of the Muhyiddin Ibn 'Arabi Society,* Vol VI, 1987.

Response to Sheer Beauty, *Beshara News Bulletin*, Summer 1985.

To Suggest a Vernacular . . ., *Beshara*, No 1, Spring 1987.

A Consideration since Assisi, *Beshara*, No 1, Spring 1987.

Union, An Address to the Symposium on Humanity, The Beshara Trust, 1979.

Great Dishes of the World in Colour, ed. Jennifer Feller, Hamlyn, London 1976. *The section on the Eastern Mediterranean is by Bulent Rauf. Each section was originally planned as a separate volume.*

Historical adviser, contributor to the script, and one of the narrators for the film *Turning*, Produced and Directed by Diane Cilento, 1975.

Unpublished: *The Last Sultans.* A history of the closing period of the Ottoman Empire.